ADELE
in SAND LAND

A TOON BOOK BY
Claude Ponti

ALSO LOOK FOR **CHICK AND CHICKIE PLAY ALL DAY** BY THE SAME AUTHOR

For my parents and for Françoise Dolto

Editorial Director & Designer: FRANÇOISE MOULY

Translation: SKEETER GRANT & FRANÇOISE MOULY

Coloring: MONIQUE RAUSCHER & CLAUDE PONTI

CLAUDE PONTI'S artwork was done in ink and watercolors.

A TOON Book™ © 2017 Claude Ponti & TOON Books, an imprint of Raw Junior, LLC, 27 Greene Street, New York, NY 10013. Originally published as "Adèle et la pelle." © 1988 Gallimard Jeunesse. All rights reserved. No part of this book may be used or reproduced in any manner whatsoever without written permission except in the case of brief quotations embodied in critical articles and reviews. TOON Graphics™, TOON Books®, LITTLE LIT® and TOON Into Reading!™ are trademarks of RAW Junior, LLC. All our books are Smyth Sewn (the highest library-quality binding available) and printed with soy-based inks on acid-free, woodfree paper harvested from responsible sources. Printed in China by C&C Offset Printing Co., Ltd. Distributed to the trade by Consortium Book Sales; orders (800) 283-3572; orderentry@perseusbooks.com; www.cbsd.com. Library of Congress Cataloging-in-Publication Data: Ponti, Claude, 1948- author, illustrator. [Adèle et la pelle. English] Adele in Sand Land : a TOON book / by Claude Ponti; translated from the French by Skeeter Grant & Françoise Mouly. New York, NY : TOON Books, 2017 Summary: Adele sits down to play in the sandbox, and embarks on a fantasy adventure involving a barefoot king, a cloud of fluffy chicks, and a dessert island. Identifiers: LCCN 2016036359 ISBN 9781943145164 (hardcover : alk. paper) Subjects: LCSH: Graphic novels CYAC: Graphic novels. | Play--Fiction. | Imagination--Fiction. | Parks--Fiction. Classification: LCC PZ7.7.P66 Ad 2017 | DDC 741.5/944--dc23 LC record available at https://lccn.loc.gov/2016036359. See our free cartoon makers, lesson plans and more at www.TOON-BOOKS.com

ISBN: 978-1-943145-16-4 (hardcover)

17 18 19 20 21 22 C&C 10 9 8 7 6 5 4 3 2 1

WWW.TOON-BOOKS.COM

Mama takes Adele to the park.

There are lots of kids in the sandbox. Lots and lots and lots of kids.

Adele's stuffed doll, Stuffy, stays with Mama. Adele looks for a place to dig.

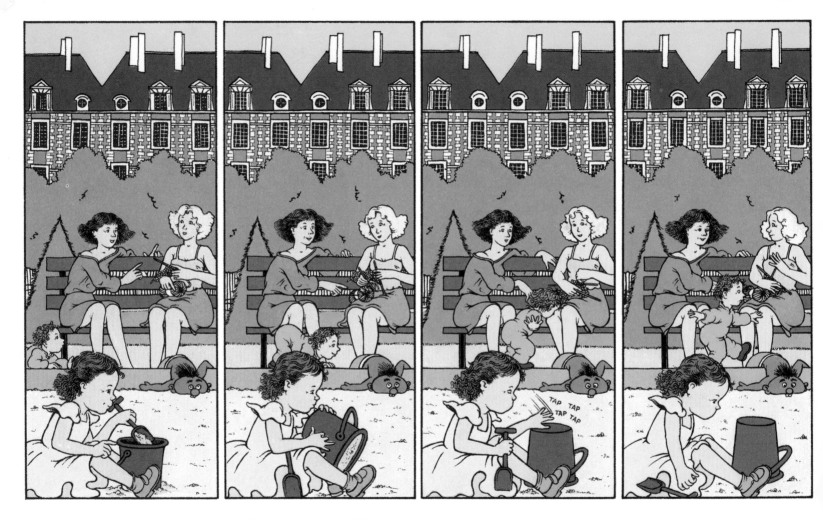

Adele fills her pail. She turns it upside down and taps.

"Who's knocking?" asks Sandy. He comes out to see.

The Masked Chickie comes out of the pail too. He says hi to Stuffy.

Sandy does the "*Hello, I'm Glad to Meet You*" dance for Adele. It's beautiful.

A Sand Dragon surprises them.

With a flick of his tongue, he eats them all up.

The friends fall and crash into cages.

A furball gets free. He says thank you and waves goodbye.

They walk on King's Road. The King likes to walk barefoot on the heads of his people.

The friends give the people books and pots and pans to cover their heads.

An angry policeman takes them to the King. The King screams, "*LISTEN TO ME!*...

I'm locking you up in a Cage Bird. No one will ever hear from you again."

Adele breaks into song, an ear-splitting song. It sets the friends free.

She grabs a fluffy cloud, a cloud of fluffy chicks.

They touch the ground lightly and tickle it.

The ground shakes with laughter and brushes them away.

They land on the ice at the top of the world.

Adele is very cold in her summer dress. Some furballs come out to say hello.

One furball says: "You helped me. Now we will help you."

The furballs make them warm and cozy. The icy snow turns into ice cream pops.

The ice melts into an ice cube. Our friends worry about being erased.

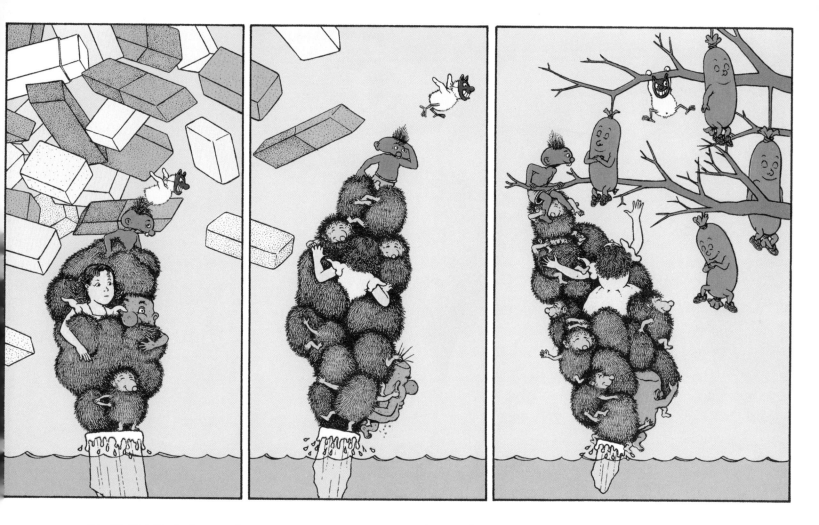

"LOOK! A hot dog tree—we're saved," Adele says. "Let's climb on."

The hot dogs say, "Don't wake up our King and Queen! They'll cook us."

"You're too cute to eat," says Adele. "Sandy is a sandman. He'll keep them asleep."

"*NOW* I'm hungry," says Adele, but finding land is as easy as pie.

They come to an island–not a desert island but a *DESSERT* island.

"Yummy! Eat up now," says Adele. "Who *KNOWS* what will happen next."

"Maybe this NOSE knows," says the Masked Chick.

"I've seen a running nose, but I never saw a flying nose," says Adele. "Let's get in."

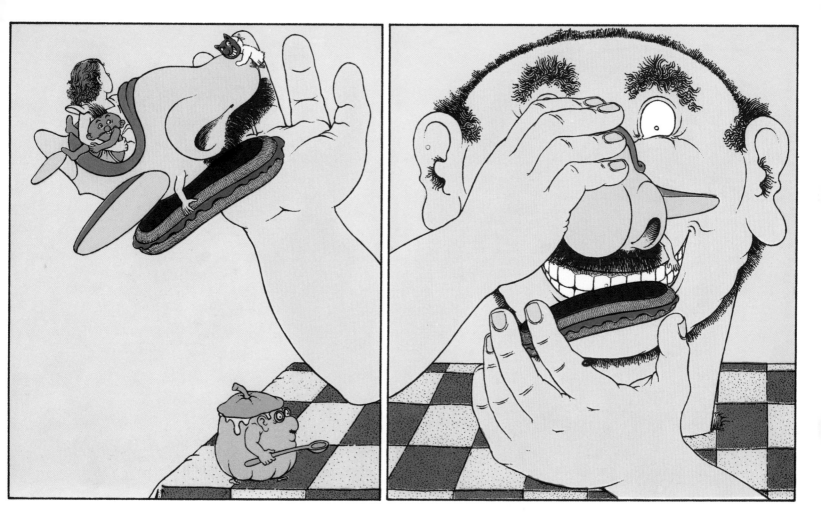

It is the nose of the giant Snack Man. It's trained to bring him sweets.

"HEY! My nose is stuffed up!" says the Snack Man.

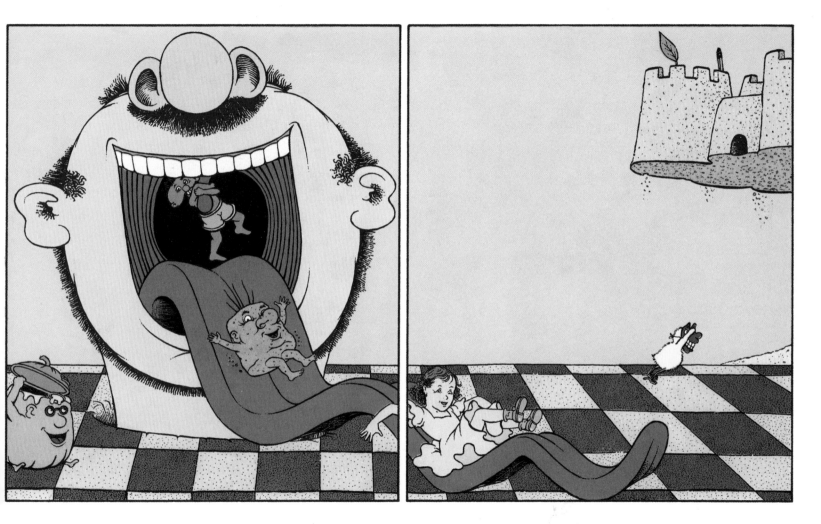

He opens his mouth to sneeze. His jaw locks and our friends slide out.

After every adventure, it's time to go home. Adele finds a tunnel.

Tunnels always take you somewhere. This one takes her back to Mama.

Mama says it's snack time, but Adele says: "No, thank you. I'm full."

ABOUT THE AUTHOR

CLAUDE PONTI is an internationally celebrated author and illustrator who lives in France. He created his first picture book, *Adèle's Album*, after the birth of his daughter Adèle in 1985 and has gone on to publish more than sixty titles for children. He fondly remembers climbing trees as a boy, looking for the best spot to sit and read a book. Now tree-climbing readers all over the world love his books. When asked what he'd most like to eat if he ever landed on Dessert Island, he said: "I'd look for a giant raspberry with a door made of pure chocolate and a white chocolate staircase. Once inside, I'd eat all the berries with warm, just-baked cookies and cold vanilla ice cream. That would make me thirsty, so I'd drink freshly-pressed orange and grape juice."

TIPS FOR PARENTS AND TEACHERS:

HOW TO READ COMICS WITH KIDS

Kids love comics! They are naturally drawn to the details in the pictures, which make them want to read the words. Comics beg for repeated readings and let both emerging and reluctant readers enjoy complex stories with a rich vocabulary. But since comics have their own grammar, here are a few tips for reading them with kids:

GUIDE YOUNG READERS: Use your finger to show your place in the text, but keep it at the bottom of the character speaking so it doesn't hide the very important facial expressions.

HAM IT UP! Think of the comic book story as a play, and don't hesitate to read with expression and intonation. Assign parts or get kids to supply the sound effects, a great way to reinforce phonics skills.

LET THEM GUESS: Comics provide lots of context for the words, so emerging readers can make informed guesses. Like jigsaw puzzles, comics ask readers to make connections, so check children's understanding by asking "What's this character thinking?" (but don't be surprised if a kid finds some of the comics' subtle details faster than you).

TALK ABOUT THE PICTURES: Point out how the artist paces the story with pauses (silent panels) or speeded-up action (a burst of short panels). Discuss how the size and shape of the panels convey meaning.

ABOVE ALL, ENJOY! There is of course never one right way to read, so go for the shared pleasure. Once children make the story happen in their imagination, they have discovered the thrill of reading, and you won't be able to stop them. At that point, just go get them more books, and more comics.

www.TOON-BOOKS.com

SEE OUR FREE ONLINE CARTOON MAKERS, LESSON PLANS, AND MUCH MORE